CW01072823

RIME

To Pat

RIME

By the star-dogged moon...

TIM LEBBON

RIME

Published in October 2018 by PS Publishing Ltd. by arrangement
with the author. All rights reserved by the author.

FIRST PS EDITION

ISBN
978-1-786363-86-2
978-1-786363-87-9 (signed edition)

Design & Layout by Michael Smith

Printed and bound in England by T.J. International

PS Publishing Ltd
Grosvenor House
1 New Road, Hornsea
HU18 1PG, England

editor@pspublishing.co.uk
www.pspublishing.co.uk

RIME

I OPEN MY EYES AND I'M STILL ALIVE. IT COMES as a blessed relief and a welcome miracle, as it has every morning since I've been here. But then I remember the reason for my survival, and what came before, and guilt lands with the force of unknown gravities. I despair at the awfulness of it all, yet I can't help but revel in my continued survival. The two emotions form the extremes of every waking hour. I am, as Luke insists on reminding me, a creature of contradictions.

As if bidden by my thinking his name—and perhaps that's true, because there are many aspects I have yet to learn about this amazing, almost unfathomable future—Luke walks through the door as if it wasn't there at all. I have seen this a dozen times since my arrival, and a dozen times I have tried, unsuccessfully, to leave the same way. For me, the door remains solid.

"Good morning," Luke says. "Shall we go out onto the balcony?"

I've tried going out there as well, but have found no way to open the wide glass walls. Luke and the woman accompanying him walk straight through. I follow, feeling no hint of resistance at all. Once outside, I glance back briefly and see myself reflected in the glass, like a ghost from the past.

I've been avoiding my reflection because it reminds me of what I've done. I see the sad, haunted man; the thin, haggard face; the long limbs, tall body, waving hair framing my sadness. Yet it's the unmistakeable glint in my eyes that troubles me most. The knowledge of a second chance.

"Shall we sit?" Luke asks, and three comfortable stools rise from the balcony's floor.

"Who's we?" I ask, looking at the woman. Like everyone I've seen here she's very beautiful, and perhaps one day soon I'll ask about that. It's one more question whose answer frightens me.

"This is Olivia," Luke says. "She's going to be your liaison for the case."

"I'm being charged, then?"

Luke's smile drops. Olivia looks away, out from the balcony and across the staggering view that I usually see only through glass. Now, being out in the open air and involved in the view itself, it almost takes my breath away. The building I'm being kept in must be over a mile high, one of seven set across the wide, flat plain. Silent aircraft drift gracefully between towers on slender wings, and huge airships sometimes cruise in from the distance, emerging from the haze to park high above and disgorge their smaller cousins.

A river flows across the plain, and the tall towers are built along its winding course. There are boats moving slowly along its length. Settlements speckle its banks, none of them large. Herds of creatures I can't identify spot the ground, moving like shadows on my eye. Birds flock and swoop, and several times one or more have landed on my balcony, cleaning their feathers or scraping their beaks on the balustrade. None fly close now, not with us sitting there. I'm not surprised. It's as if they know who I am.

"I don't think there was ever any doubt," Olivia says. "You're responsible for the deaths of seventeen million people."

She has no real expression as she states that stark fact. I can't read her at all. I'm already doubting that they're even human.

"You can't kill those that are already dead," I say.

Olivia sighs and looks away, as if I'm already a lost cause.

"That's not what the ship's records hint at," Luke says. He's only repeating what he's stated a dozen times before.

"You told me you're not sure what they show. That they're so old, you're having trouble accessing them."

Luke glances at Olivia and shrugs. It makes no difference. I know the truth, however unknowable it is.

I stand and lean on the balustrade, looking down. The height is dizzying, barely visible vehicles crawling around the base of the tower like ants, wisps of cloud drifting past below. I wonder if there are real ants on this world. Once, several days earlier, I awoke to find a low cloud layer obscuring the entire landscape, only the protruding tower tops visible, sunlight making the cloudscape glow with a gorgeous, unnatural light. It was beautiful, but didn't make me feel any more lonely than I already am.

I wonder if they're worried that I'll throw myself from the balcony. I suspect there are safety measures I can't see. And even if there aren't, I would only be ridding them of an awkward, unprecedented problem.

"It wasn't my fault," I say, tears burning my eyes because I know, I *know*, that all of it was.

"Tell Olivia what you told me," Luke says.

I laugh. "What, so it can become my defence?"

"Just so that I know," she says. "Luke thinks..." She glances at Luke, and it's the first time I've seen anything approaching doubt, uncertainty, humanity. It confuses me even more.

"I've told her you have an amazing story," Luke says.

I look out over that vast, incredible landscape once more, and wonder if I'll ever feel that I've reached the end of my journey.

That day, like every other day of my life, I rose at dawn. Dawn was dictated by the ship's Environmentals, and it hadn't changed in a long, long time. My father woke at dawn, and his father, and as far as I'm aware my great-great-grandfather was up and about just as Cradle started to slowly turn on the lights. He wrote in his journal that there were 'things to do'. I always laughed at that. So many things to do.

Geena had already left. Her side of the bed was cool, and when I felt her coffee cup in our small galley, it was only vaguely warm. The same temperature, perhaps, as our failing relationship. Neither of us could really put a finger on what was going wrong, and we still felt like friends. It was strange.

We were shipborn, of course. Seventh generation. Geena had read lots about how that might be detrimental to our ability to form relationships. I think perhaps her just reading about relationship difficulties caused them.

She was six months pregnant by then. Generation eight was already growing throughout Cradle, and our child would form part of that. We had yet to discuss which part— MediTech after Geena; or Edge, following in my footsteps. Our child would have to be allocated soon, but that was a conversation I had no wish to initiate.

Geena was something of a rebel, and she believed that we were all prisoners.

She worked in the Nurseries. Geena was one of those whose job it was to ensure they were maintained, and that their contents—those countless people in cryo-sleep— remained fit and healthy. Most days she had to travel to a Nursery where an alert had started pulsing, and on the worst days she had to shut down one, or even two tubes. She hated doing that. Said it was like killing them—though it really wasn't—and that they should have some sort of funeral. They never did, though. They were left in the tubes until they softened, then jettisoned into recycling.

Geena believed that we were as much prisoners as them. I never really understood that outlook. They were here voluntarily, and we were simply continuing what our ancestors had been tasked with. None of what we did was about being trapped.

That day, I washed and dressed and started out towards Edge, and all the time I was wondering what we would say to each other later. I was planning a different evening. A movie, perhaps, or a trip out to Edge to see the stars. I saw them every day, but for Geena it was always a fresh experience.

Anything, other than what normally happened. Back to our cabin, food, some aimless talk, and then Geena burying herself in history holos. We all knew about Earth, and what had happened, and why we were on Cradle, and most of us appreciated that we were pioneers on humanity's greatest adventure. Geena saw things in a different light. As far as she was concerned, we should have never given up hope.

I travelled out to Edge in a rail tube with several other crew members absorbed in their own thoughts. The trip took twenty minutes, then we went our separate ways. It was all very familiar, very normal, just what I had been doing virtually every day for the past four years. Prior to that I was an Environmental technician for eight years. Career changes kept us fresh. Cradle told us that. Cradle told us everything.

Edge was a place and profession that some people craved, and some feared with every beat of their heart. I loved it, I think because it was an extreme in every sense of the word. The edge of our existence, it was also the place where danger pressed in close to the contained environment in which we lived. Cradle was huge—too huge to contemplate other than in the vaguest of terms—but out at Edge, I saw the end of Cradle and the beginning of infinity.

I stood and looked out at the stars that morning, as I did every morning, and wondered.

I had a scheduled checklist to go through before I could perform a more random inspection. My portion of Edge covered a very defined extent of Cradle's outer hull. Eight hundred metres north to south, section seventeen. Six hundred metres east to west, section fourteen. It incorporated three antenna arrays, two external access ports containing emergency escape craft, and several viewing platforms. There was also one plasma cannon enclosure.

From my section's dedicated control room I checked a whole range of statuses. Hull integrity, of course, as well as a selection of system readings, anomalies, and other conditions that never, ever changed. That day I was also scheduled to run diagnostics on the two escape craft. Before I got to that I decided to make a coffee and go out onto one of the viewing platforms.

It protruded from Edge a little, just enough to make me feel like I was above and away from things. The hull disappeared north and south almost as far as I could see, broken at regular intervals by other platforms in different sections. They were too far away to see whether they contained people also watching me. I could have used communicators, but at moments like this I quite liked being alone. If any other Edge techs were out there, I guessed they did too.

South, thousands of metres away, I could just make out the bulge of Drive. Over ten thousand metres north was Bridge. I'd never been there, though I knew a couple of other Edge techs who'd been Bridge staff in their younger days. They didn't talk about it much. I guess there wasn't much for them to do with the whole ship under the control of Cradle's ever-expanding, ever learning AI.

East and west, the ship curved away towards the horizon, and it was only these gradual curves that gave any sense of scale. That, and the stars. I felt that I could sit and stare at them for hours, though I hardly ever did.

That day, wandering around the viewing platform with coffee going cold in my cup, I looked out at the stars and saw *them*.

There were five.

I couldn't understand what I was seeing. How could I? They were beyond my experience, and outside of anything anyone had ever encountered before. I stared for a while, then accessed a comm-port and queried Cradle.

"I've been watching them for seven hours," Cradle said.

"What are they?" I asked.

"Unknown."

"Ships? Dust clouds? Living organisms?"

"Composition unknown."

"Have they tried to communicate?"

"Unknown."

"Unknown? Surely you'd know if they tried to comm-unicate?"

"Unknown. Like I said." Cradle was sometimes as cranky as its three-thousand-strong skeleton crew. I didn't know whether the AI had been designed that way, or had grown prickly over the several centuries it had already existed, but I'd never liked that aspect of the ship. Its fake humanity. Its alien intelligence. Even though it was all I'd ever known, part of me still understood that it wasn't right. It was one thing that Geena and I had agreed upon from the start.

"Distance?"

"Unknown."

"Huh. Right." I left the comm-port open and walked closer to the observation portal. There was now only half a metre of clear composite between me and eternity, and marring that view were those five strange, graceful, diaphanous shapes. They were amazing, and terrifying. I shivered. They were the first real things I'd ever seen beyond the ship, other than the countless specks of stars and, once, the distant smear of a comet. I understood that there was much more out there than this ship I'd been born into and upon which I was destined to die, but actually *seeing* more was a profound experience.

"Suggested action?" I whispered.

"Caution," Cradle said. "All eventualities require consideration."

"Eventualities?"

"The shapes have matched our direction and velocity. That suggests sentience."

"And you've no idea how big they are, or how far away?"

"Still computing."

I had a dozen responses to that, but none felt quite adequate. The last thing I wanted to hear in Cradle's voice was fear. Could an AI even be afraid? That was not something I had any wish to discover. Cradle had always been there, the ship and its mind, a constant presence containing and nursing me through life. And although the whole crew was required to learn human history and context during their childhood, for many of us the ship remained close to a god.

Now, perhaps I was looking at others.

"Cannon arrays activated," Cradle said. Its voice sounded quieter, and not because I was further away from the comm-port.

"Really?" I asked. The plasma cannon enclosure in my section had not been opened or entered in years. I had never been in there, even though it was my responsibility to check its systems. I did so remotely. Everything was remote, and I only performed visual checks of areas such as this observation platform because it pleased me to do so.

I had never been drawn to the plasma cannon enclosure. It wasn't a part of the ship I had ever thought I'd have to use.

"You should go there," Cradle said.

"Me?" It was shock more than surprise. I knew the protocols, even before Cradle reminded me of them.

I looked north and east across the body of the ship, cold blue hull smooth and virtually featureless between me and the cannon array. It was a half-spherical hump three hundred metres away. It appeared benign, yet I was aware of the power it could unleash.

"Rail rube seven-A ready," Cradle said. "I'd advise haste."

"Why do you . . . ?" I trailed off.

I realised that they were coming closer.

As they moved, their shapes became more apparent. I felt sick with dread and wonder. I backed up to the comm-port and stroked the screen, opening all channels and taking comfort from the flood of excited, terrified chatter.

"Are you seeing this?" I asked my colleagues across the ship, other Edge-techs on this side who were all now looking in the same direction. Mine was one of a hundred voices filled with wonder, disbelief, and sometimes terror.

I thought of Geena and our unborn child. I reached out to the screen again.

"Really. It's time to move." Cradle sounded insistent.

"I want to tell—"

"The situation is known ship-wide."

The door behind me whispered open and the viewing windows hazed opaque, all but blocking my view.

"Do they mean us harm?" I asked.

"Beats me," Cradle said. I had never heard it sounding so human.

I hurried through to the designated rail-tube, and moments later was disgorged close to the cannon array. I entered the code and the door whisked open. It ground on its runners, sealed with dust and time. The interior was stark and functional, even more so than other parts of Cradle's operational areas, and I took a moment looking around at the place I had never been. I knew how it worked, because we all had to spend time in the sim-pods as children, and again as adults when we were assigned certain posts. But there was a smell to the place, a feel, that no sim-pod could convey, and which I found distasteful.

"I've taken the liberty of firing up all systems," Cradle said.

"Good, yeah, thanks." It was not only talking to me. Across the surface of the massive ship, cannon arrays would be opening like weeping blisters, turning to face the approaching objects, cannons extruding from their protective sheaths and flowing with coolant, starting to pulse with the potential destruction held deep in their individual reactors.

I sat in the control seat and touched a screen, drawing all the controls in around my body. Everything settled at the optimum distance, moving as I moved, displaying information wherever I looked. It was like wearing a suit without anything actually touching my skin.

"Visuals," I said, and several display screens formed in front of me, combining to show one wide, uninterrupted view of space.

They had come much, much closer. I gasped, then held my breath as the first of the massive objects seemed to drift right over my cannon array and disappear out of sight.

11

They had wings.

"Cradle—" I said, but a loud hissing sound swamped my voice. For a few seconds all systems buzzed and flashed, screens flickering and hissing, my seat vibrating.

Then everything in the cannon array—and as far as I knew, every system all across the ship—faded away to nothing.

On a ship containing three hundred crew and many millions of sleeping souls, for the first time ever, I felt alone.

"Would you like to go for a walk?"

It's only Olivia with me this time, and her question takes me by surprise. Though they're being nice to me, it's never been a secret that I'm a prisoner in these rooms. That rarely concerns me. Now, the idea of getting outside and away from the same four walls is incredibly attractive. Perhaps I might even feel grass beneath my feet.

Geena always said that experience had been stolen from us.

I glance at Olivia and she's smiling. It's tentative, as if she's unsure whether I can accept anyone feeling or appearing happy around me. My recounting of the story has only just begun, but everyone already knows something of how it ends.

"I'd like that."

She nods, relieved, and heads out to the balcony. I feel a flush of disappointment.

"Oh. I thought you meant..."

A craft rises from out of sight below. It's a simple platform with rails, and whatever power source drives it is hidden beneath swept metal skirting. Olivia glances back, one eyebrow raised, and then steps up onto the balcony wall. One more step and she is on board, waiting for me. The craft makes very little noise. It reminds me of the constant, almost unnoticeable background hum of Cradle.

Once I'm with her, Olivia performs several subtle gestures with her left hand and the platform drops away, sweeping out from the building and down towards the plain. There is no breeze, very little sound, and hardly any sense of movement. Even so, she remains silent. She knows how much I want to take this in, and her consideration surprises me as much as ever. If she truly sees me as a mass murderer, she is very good at hiding her thoughts.

The tower recedes behind us, seemingly growing higher as we drop away. I keep focussed on my rooms, my balcony, but soon it is lost from view. The structure is far wider and taller than I thought, mostly regular in shape apart from several sweeping protuberances around the tower's head, far higher than my own rooms. They remind me of wings, and that reminds me of Cradle and what happened, and I turn away and look down. We are already close to the ground, and this low there are many other craft drifting to and fro. There don't seem to be any defined routes, yet every aircraft shifts in a graceful dance, never drawing too close to those around them.

"There's a lovely path along the river," Olivia says. "The bluebells will be out now."

"Sounds good."

She makes another gesture and the craft veers to the left, dropping down and landing softly at the edge of a field of bright yellow blooms. Several creatures scamper away, hiding in the undergrowth and watching us with glittering, intelligent eyes. I think perhaps they are rabbits.

13

"We'll have company, I'm afraid," Olivia says. Two small objects rise from the surface of the craft, coalescing into shiny globes that draw close to us, so close that I can see my own distorted reflection in them both. I nod. I understand without her having to tell me that these are some sort of robot guards. If I run, I won't get far.

They must know by now that the last thing I want to do is run.

We step down from the platform onto the ground, and I gasp. *This is it*, I think. *I really am standing on the ground.* I slip off my sandals and clench my toes in the grass.

"I'll arrange for some food to be brought out to us," she says. "Shall we walk a little? You'll have to go back to your rooms later, but we have a while."

"And meantime I continue my story, right?"

"I'm trying to help," she says.

I nod and smile. I know she is, and it's unfair of me to suggest otherwise. I can't blame them for thinking of me as a monster.

Telling my story is the only way to defend myself. There are decisions, sacrifices, that systems and computers—even an AI like Cradle—can never truly understand.

It's all about being human.

I stare at Olivia, and not for the first time I wonder if she is.

I was trapped in the cannon array. Weapon systems were still online, but I was completely isolated. No contact with Cradle, no channels open to other arrays, or the Bridge, or anywhere else. Just me and the weapon screens, the cannon controls, and the weapon's reactor status indicators.

There was also the view outside, with those things drifting with us, passing overhead, and buzzing Cradle.

They were massive. They must have been, to have been visible from so far away. The wings captured starlight and twisted, curled, flexed. Their bodies were slender and difficult to discern, one moment appearing solid, the next diaphanous. Sometimes the five shapes were similar, and then the next moment they were individual and unique, examples of something I had yet to fully understand. Animals? Gas? Illusions? Cradle had said it didn't know, and now it was down to me to decide. I'd never been so alone.

I locked the cannon onto one of the objects and hovered my hand over the activation screen.

Another shape peeled off to the south and closed in quickly, swooping down and out of sight around Cradle's curving hull.

"Hello?" I said, touching the all-channels screen. "Anyone out there? Can anyone hear me?" I switched channels, sub-vocalised a code, and tried again. "Geena? Can you hear me?" She would be down in Cradle's belly, several kilometres away where countless people slept time away in cryo-tubes. She kept them well. None of them would ever know her—we would all die of old age before we even reached our destination—but she cared for them nonetheless. They were humanity's future.

"Geena?" I shouted, knowing it would do no good. I tried the cannon array access controls again. Then one more attempt to communicate with Cradle.

It should hear me!

"Cradle? Cradle!"

Maybe it's ignoring me.

It should have worked. When all hard systems were down, we were all fitted with smart pods deep inside our left ears through which we could access the Cradle AI at any time, and from any place.

Except now.

I felt abandoned, and imagined every other crew member struggling with the same problem. Desperate to not be alone anymore, while those things—

Two swept in close together, almost dancing with each other as they drifted in from the north. One peeled off and disappeared from my sight, curving quickly around the ship's hull. The other slowed to a virtual halt.

It might have been in touching distance, or ten kilometres away. I stared, hand still hovering over the cannon activator. I locked on. I was shaking. The scanner glowed green and awaited my one, final touch.

Watching it, I also felt the thing watching me.

"Hello?" I asked. No one, nothing answered. Each of us was now alone, vulnerable, and ever since birth we had all been part of a team, connected permanently to Cradle and each other via the smart pods. We were a unit that worked together, and being cut off like this could only be bad. The sense of isolation was crippling.

They must have done this on purpose.

It's an attack, I thought. *Maybe they've killed everyone else on the ship and that's why I can't hear or communicate with anyone. Maybe they've murdered Cradle.*

Almost without thinking, almost of its own accord, my hand lowered and stroked across the screen.

My senses were flooded with light as the whole array shuddered around me. A loud thump punched at my ears and stole my breath. The shaking soon settled, but my vision took longer, swimming with blooming palettes of red and orange like exploding suns. I blinked and pressed my hands to my eyes. When I took them away, everything had changed.

Silence hung heavier over the interior of my cannon array. I felt watched, the centre of attention, no longer cut off but the focus of absolutely everything.

Outside the ship, I began to see what I had done.

The thing had been shattered by the single plasma cannon blast. It floated away from Cradle, one vast wing spinning gracefully aside from its body, a haze of smaller debris spreading from the impact point. Broken, its body now looked more solid than ever.

I frowned. Tears pressed at my eyes. *What have I done?* The shape was receding, shoved away from the Cradle by the force of the plasma bloom, and suddenly the other four objects swooped in to surround it. They reached for it with incredibly fine tendrils, invisible until now. They moved in even closer, hiding the damaged thing with their own flexing wings.

For a moment I imagined their attention turned on me. I was still the focus, the centre of whatever terrible thing had happened, and I tried to retreat into myself, curling up in my seat and crying out as their vast intelligences moved across and through me. Then they cast me aside, and in the blink of an eye they swept away, a blur across the darkness, a pale dot no brighter than a distant star, and then nothing.

Shivering and hugging myself, I stared after them.

"—back online," Cradle said, the AI's familiar voice startling me. "System checks commencing. Oh. There seems to be a problem."

Cradle was speaking to us all.

"I know how difficult this next part must be," Olivia says. "After all, Geena..."

The name of my love rings hollow to me. I've repeated it so many times to myself since waking, out loud and in my mind, that it has ceased being a real word and become a sound, like a sigh or a sob. Hearing it spoken by someone else, it sounds like a foreign language.

"It's not that," I say. We're sitting on a slight rise around which the river curves. An ox-bow lake, I remember from Earth-lessons on the ship. The gentle slopes are spiked with tall, thin trees, their canopies alive with twittering birds and hundreds of butterflies. Bees and other insects buzz and speckle the air. I almost recognise some of the birds, and some of the butterfly species might be familiar. An insect with six wings lands on my hand, and even as it sinks its proboscis into the flesh between thumb and forefinger, I do not swat it or flick it away.

How can I? It's alive, and more amazing than anything humankind has ever created or achieved.

Even coming here.

"It's just that I feel so far away from home," I say. "So far away from everything."

"This is your home now," she says. There's a tenderness to her voice, one that I've never heard in a machine. Cradle could joke and mock, sound stern or flat, but I had never heard true emotion in the AI's voice, only an impersonation. Geena and I had argued about that. She'd always believed that the ship was as alive as any of us. If that *were* true, then that meant one more death on my hands.

I study the insect feeding on my blood. True life. Nothing artificial there.

"My home, and yet I'll be on trial for mass murder."

"Not murder."

I shrug. "Same thing."

"Not at all. It's ... a formality."

I laugh, and it feels good. I haven't laughed like that for some time, not from the belly. Maybe it's the fresh air. Olivia seems confused at my reaction.

"After coming so far," I say, waving one hand as I recover from my guffaw. "So far, so long, only to find you made it here before me. It's all too much." I hold my head. "I'm really not sure we're built to accept such extreme times and distances."

I think of that face staring at me, a reflection of my own and yet knowing and understanding so much more. And I *know* this is true. We're not wired to understand any of this.

No one has talked much about the past—not Luke, and certainly not Olivia. I assume it's because their task is to extract as much of the truth out of me as they can. Perhaps after all this time they really do feel sorry for me.

Cradle had been travelling for three hundred years by the time I was born, fleeing a dying Earth and bearing hope for the future of humanity. Its journey had another four hundred years to go before reaching its intended destination, a Goldilocks planet in the Canis Major constellation. Mine was one of the generations destined to live their lives ensuring that those sleeping millions arrived there safe and sound. During that three hundred years, technology must have advanced at a huge rate. Faster ships were built, powered by more effective star drives. Ambition and the need to reach the stars grew. Sometime during our travels we were overtaken, and these others arrived on the planet long before we were ever due.

Cradle must have become a sad, guilty memory for those new settlers.

I was never meant to feel grass between my toes, or the prick of an insect's bite, or to see the sweep of this mighty river eroding its way through time on a planet almost a hundred light years from Earth.

"Your story is amazing," Olivia says, and I realise then that she doesn't believe me. What I don't understand is why. This new planet, with its vast swathes of life, means that the universe is singing with alien species.

If she can see this six-winged insect on my hand, why can she not believe in space angels?

"You've only heard the beginning," I say. The insect flits away from my hand. I hope that my blood nurtures it.

My first thought was, *What have I done?*
My second: *Geena!*

I rose from my seat, unsteady on my feet, and staggered to the door. It failed to open, and I had to stroke the manual pad three times before it worked. Out in the hallway, I sensed that something was terribly wrong. *There seems to be a problem*, Cradle had said, but it had yet to reveal what that problem was.

I paused, standing still and trying to make out exactly what was amiss. The ship hummed and vibrated as usual. But there was more air movement than normal—somewhere, too many doors were open. When I approached a comm-point and activated the screen, a subtle red warning light pulsed across the hologram display.

"What's the problem?" I asked, and the display changed.

On the left was a selection of status updates, most of them green. But a very important one glowed red.

Drive: suspended.

I frowned. Cradle operated under a continuous, very subtle acceleration—minimal fuel required, an almost imperceptible shove—intended over the centuries to shove the craft to a significant percentage of the speed of light. That drive function was now halted. Cradle continued to move incredibly quickly, but we were no longer accelerating.

On the right side of the display, the real problem began to flash.

Cryo facility: system crash.

"Oh, my God." I didn't believe in God. Few of the crew did, born as we were into a culture and lifestyle of pure science. But ancient learnings were available to us all, as was the terminology of our ancestors. There were always exceptions, and Geena was one of them. Her faith bemused and fascinated me, and I wondered what she would think about what I had done and who, or what, I had killed.

Now, the sleepers were waking. *All* of them.

My heart missed a beat. The enormity of what this represented could not hit home. It was too vast, and too unbelievable.

"Cradle, please elaborate on cryo system crash."

"The whole system has failed," Cradle said. "Cryo generators have lost power, and pods are coming offline in their thousands."

"How? What about the failsafes?" I knew from discussions with Geena that the cryo systems were the most protected on the ship, with three independently powered and routed failsafes for each nursery.

"Outside influence. All failsafes have failed."

"Those things."

"Specifically, I believe it was the one you killed."

I tried to absorb all of this. It was too much, too difficult. *Geena is down there*, I thought, because she was involved in the constant monitoring of the sleepers' health. She would be frantic right now, trying to figure out how she could help while the techs were doing their best to put right whatever had gone wrong.

Outside influence.

I wondered if she already knew what I had done.

"How long until they're fully awake?" I asked. There would be a thousand people asking Cradle a thousand questions all over the ship, and it would be answering each and every one in a personal manner. That was the nature of an AI. For me, it was the aspect that made it seem so un-natural.

I had never known exactly how many sleeping people we carried. They were cargo, and as I would never actually meet any of them I had never considered them as living, breathing entities. Someone had once told me we carried about three million souls, their lives suspended in time. Geena estimated more like nine million. No one but Cradle knew for sure, because only Cradle was in charge of the whole ship. It was both craft and captain.

"They are not waking," Cradle said.

"What?" I didn't really hear what it had said. The idea of millions of people surfacing from cryo sleep at the same time, that mysterious pausing of life, and suddenly coming awake was horrendous. It was disastrous. Cradle was built to support several thousand crew, not several million confused, weak, wandering souls.

22

They would be naked. Cold. Hungry.

"They're dying," Cradle said.

My heart jumped, fluttered, as if to remind me of the fragility of life.

"Dying?"

"Cryo system has crashed. The waking process is as complex as the processes used to put them into suspension. The whole system has failed. The suspension has ended, and the waking protocol has thus not initiated. They are no longer asleep."

"They're all dead?"

"As good as."

"As good as? What the fuck does that mean? You're an AI, you don't use terms like that. That doesn't actually mean anything."

"I'm an intelligence," Cradle said. "I'm upset."

"Upset," I whispered.

"I'm doing my best, you must know that," Cradle said. "But all indicators point to it being hopeless. I think what you did—"

"For fuck's sake, this isn't my fault!"

"You're the only Edge-tech who fired a plasma blast," Cradle said. "For fuck's sake."

I ran. I needed to find Geena. I couldn't understand or comprehend what was happening. It was all too much, too monumental, too disastrous. Everything I knew had changed in an instant, and the awful idea that I had caused that change pressed in around me. I felt as if the atmospheric pressure had suddenly increased—my ears were compressed, my surroundings distant. I was panicking. Nothing could have prepared me for this, no amount of routine disaster training that we undertook every so often. No one had really expected anything to ever go wrong.

I fled my section of Edge, jumping onto a rail tube and instructing it to take me in towards the Core. From there I could go south, three thousand metres to where Geena's MediTech headquarters was nestled above the fifth of the great cryo halls. I had only been there a couple of times before, and I tried to imagine what might be happening there now, in that vast chamber where humanity's hope was meant to sleep away this desperate, incredible journey.

I changed rail tubes, and on the next one there were three people already seated. I knew one of them, a horticultural engineer called Bellamy. He'd worked on one of the central farms since he was a child, tending crops and ensuring that we had access to the fresh foods—fruit, vegetables, modified meat growths—that kept us all alive. He was a cheerful old man now, someone who loved his job and rarely saw a downside to anything.

He stared at me as I boarded. I took a set opposite him and the two others, nodded, glanced away. Bellamy continued to stare.

"What?" I asked.

"You," he said. That was all. I held out my hands, eyebrows raised, inviting elaboration. He snorted and looked away.

"They might have been a threat," I said. It sounded weak, even to me.

"They are now," one of the others replied. She was wearing an Environment uniform. I could not recall ever seeing her before. Maybe she had come down from the north, close to Bridge. Some of the three hundred crew moved and worked in very different circles, and it was entirely possible to spend a lifetime on Cradle without seeing and knowing everyone.

"They did something," I said. "Crashed our comm systems, isolated us."

"Maybe they thought *we* were a threat," Bellamy said.

"We were," the woman replied.

"No," I said, but it sounded pathetic. I couldn't justify my actions. I could barely even explain them. I tried to recall the act of opening fire, what I had felt and thought beforehand, why I had done it, but everything was vague. Maybe the communications breakdown had made me feel like a frightened child, separated from its parents for the first time ever, but that was no excuse for the violence I had wrought.

"I'm sorry," I said. I realised that everyone throughout the ship would know that it was me. Cradle must have issued an announcement.

"I might have done the same," the other man with Bellamy and the woman said.

"I wouldn't," Bellamy said. "This was something we've wondered about for years, ever since Cradle began its journey. The possibility of encountering alien life. It wasn't our mission, but it was our hope. It should have been wonderful."

His words hung heavy, and at the first opportunity I exited the rail tube and waited for another.

Close to the Core, I started making my way south. Every rail-tube was busy, filled with crew members bustling back and forth. Not all of them seemed to recognise me, but those who did only stared. The weight of their silent accusations bore me down.

At a main station I went to a comm-port and tried to locate Geena. I found her implant quickly. In my confusion and uncertainty I'd travelled past where she worked. I tried to signal her but her implant remained inactive. She didn't want to talk to me. The idea was horrible. I hoped it was because she was incredibly busy, her and every other Medi-Tech struggling to save the millions of lives.

How selfish am I? I thought. Right then, the idea of a small room and a closed door seemed so inviting.

I scanned system updates and paused.

"Cradle?"

"I'm here."

"What's happening?"

"One of them is still with us. It's nestled around Bridge."

"Still with us," I echoed. "Do we have visuals?"

An image flashed onto the comm-port's screen. It must have been from several kilometres along the ship, magnified, and it showed one of those huge alien creatures splayed across Cradle's nose section. Wings tucked in, body laid lengthways, its many tendril-like limbs probed delicately across the ship, touching here, stroking there, never remaining in the same place for long.

"What does it want?" I asked.

"I'm not sure," Cradle said.

"Maybe it doesn't understand."

Cradle did not reply. I watched the thing, and I could not help feeling that, somehow, it also watched me.

"It just spoke," Cradle said.

"What? When? What did it say?"

"Three seconds ago. It asked for you."

"I'd like to go back to my room now," I say. "Will that platform thing take us? Can you call it back?"

"I was just about to arrange some food," Olivia said. She sounds disappointed.

"In my room. I'd like it there." A strange feeling has come over me. The river is too deep, the plain too wide, the towers dotted across the landscape far too tall. I have spent my whole life in space, but this expansive landscape is suddenly way too large.

A small room, I think, *with a closed door*.

Olivia signals the platform to return and we mount it together. I hold on and close my eyes, barely feeling the movement as we lift off once again into the sky. Opening my eyes a few moments later, I'm just in time to watch us docking with my balcony. The two small, floating drones are still with us, but they sink back down into the platform as it drops away.

Olivia indicates a spread of food laid out on a small table. Dried meats, figs, fresh bread, olives, several fruits I know and a couple I do not, I am shocked once more at the selection. Food on Cradle had been healthy but quite basic, designed more for its nutritional value than for the enjoyment of those who ate it. I feel bad even looking at this. I should not be the only one from Cradle eating it.

"It would help if there were proof," Olivia says.

"It would help if you believed me."

"I do!" she says. "Honestly, I believe you!"

"Methinks she doth protest too much."

"I'm sorry?"

I smile and shake my head. Perhaps with the speed they'd travelled here, so much more than a dying Earth had been left behind.

"My escape craft," I say. "Its computer. Surely it carries Cradle's testimony?"

"The contents are sparse," Olivia says. She smiles apologetically. "Sorry, computers aren't really my field. Luke deals in antiquities, he can tell you more."

The door whispers open and Luke enters. It's been a day since I've seen him, and I'm pleased at his presence. These are the only two people I know. Alone in the universe, I am now a man without friends or loved ones. I try to bury the idea that they're not quite human.

"How much did the escape craft tell you?" I ask.

"Hello to you, too," Luke says, smiling.

I frown. He's talking niceties, while I'm facing trial for the deaths of millions. *Countless* millions. I think of the shapes and shadows, the huddled bodies and blank faces devoid of hope, humour or humanity. In my mind's eye, their expressions are still there, frozen for eternity. Their blankness is full of blame.

"I'm telling the truth," I say. "All of it. Every word, every terrible thing, it all happened."

Neither of them replies.

"So, the escape ship computer?" I ask.

"There wasn't much," Luke says. He strolls to the table and plucks up a slice of dried meat and a fig. He peruses the dips and chutneys, then opts for eating it plain. As he chews, he pours himself a glass of water.

"But it backs up my story?" I ask.

"Well, some of it." He sighs and sits down. "The Cradle AI... it sort of went down with the ship." He smiles.

"It's not funny," I say. "Nothing about this is amusing."

His face grows stern. "Oh, I know that. Olivia and I have the task of debriefing you, and the responsibility is heavy on—"

"Heavy?" I ask, aghast. A hand touches my arm. Olivia. For a couple of seconds I relish the contact, then I shake her off and walk towards the window. There's a rustle of movement behind me, and Luke appears by my side.

"I don't mean to make light of any of this," he says. "But look at it from our point of view. You arrive in orbit and you're . . . almost a legend, millennia old. We lost contact with Cradle centuries ago, and ever since then we've believed it lost. A tragedy, a disaster, but no more so than what Cradle was fleeing. Now you're here with your amazing story and we have to do this right. We have to make sure that every aspect is covered. It's difficult for Olivia and me. Though not, I'll admit, as difficult as it must be for you."

"You have no idea," I say.

"No."

"So the escape ship?" I prompt.

"Cradle left no part of its programming in the escape craft. Its systems were autonomous. There's a log that records the abandoning of Cradle. One passenger—you—in a ship designed for over a hundred. But other than that we have very little objective information. Our own AIs are interrogating the systems further, to see if there are loops or subroutines containing more information, but the systems are *very* old. We're not anticipating much progress."

"I just can't believe I made it here, so far away from Earth, and I'm the only one. If it wasn't so bloody tragic, some might see it as a triumph."

"What?" Olivia whispers.

"I was never meant to be anywhere like this. Do you understand that? I was supposed to be born, live out my life, and die in service of Cradle and its cargo, all in deep space. That doesn't matter—it *didn't* matter—because it's all I'd have known, and conditions for me and the rest of the crew were fine. We knew our duties." I look at the array of food and think of simpler times.

Olivia and Luke are conversing in whispers, so I walk out onto the balcony, away from them and into my own company once more. I'd spent centuries asleep, alone on the escape ship, and I'm not sure I'll feel at home among other people ever again. Centuries asleep, but to me those terrible events still feel like mere days ago.

The loss of Geena is equally fresh.

"Don't you understand the pain I'm in?" I whisper. I intend the words purely for myself, but Olivia is beside me. She touches my arm again, and this time I do not shake her off.

"We're trying," she says. "But... where do you think you are?"

The question comes as a shock. At first I barely understand. I look out across the wide, daunting landscape and see the progress and growth that has been accomplished. While I slept, the rest of humanity did not. They strove to survive, fought against hardships, and eventually triumphed. Perhaps their ships had even passed within a light year or two of my escape craft as they overtook humanity's last hope, its greatest adventure. The Cradle of its new beginning, now empty and dead.

"I know where I am," I say.

"But where do you *think* you are?"

"I reached Canis Major," I say. "After so long. Three hundred years, then the disaster, then however much longer I was in cryo sleep on the escape ship."

"No," Olivia says. She looks troubled, and glancing back at Luke I can see his pale face, his own confusion.

"What?" I ask

"You're on Earth," she says.

I shake my head. It's not possible. Earth was back in the past, its dying our reason for leaving in the first place. We'd all learned about it as our place of origin, but also our reason for leaving—that Earth could no longer sustain humanity. Poisoned seas, toxic atmosphere, a sun's deadly rays, flooded lowlands, overgrown populations destined to die from starvation, radiation poisoning or pandemics. It was a terrible end to our home planet, and a valuable lesson to carry onwards to our new home in Canis Major.

Earth was not part of me, and never would be.

"Yes," she said.

"But . . . " I raise my hand and sweep it from left to right, as if to wipe out the view.

"We made it better," she says. "Science leapt forward. Nano-tech helped clean the air. Population control became a powerful issue. Insect farming fought famine. Lots of other stuff I don't even understand."

"Your escape ship brought you home," Luke says.

"Home?" I have never felt so far away.

"We suspect that Cradle changed the programming. Rather than complete the journey to Canis Major, after the tragedy it sent you back to Earth. We're trying to find out why."

"But the trajectories, the distances, the time. All those calculations. It's impossible."

"Only vastly improbable," Olivia says. She's still holding my arm, and now she moves in closer and embraces me. I feel her warmth. I smell her breath, sense her heartbeat against my back, and I know at last that she really is human. My suspicions about her and Luke fade away, feeling foolish and insignificant.

"How long?" I ask.

"We think almost three thousand years," she says. "But imagine, if you *had* gone on to Canis Major, you'd have been alone forever."

I close my eyes and remember Cradle, its multitude of dead, and the woman I still love. I have never felt as alone as I do now.

I wanted to see Geena before I went north to Bridge. With the weight of Cradle and everyone in it on my shoulders, it was still my loved one at the forefront of my mind.

Cradle cleared a rail tube route for me so that I didn't have to stop at waypoints or change tubes. My journey would be quick, so I didn't have too much time to think about what I'd do when I reached my destination.

After only several minutes, I stopped.

"What's happening?" Cradle asked.

"I need to see Geena."

"She doesn't matter right now."

"You're a machine. You have no idea what you're saying." I opened the tube door and stepped onto the platform. It was eerily quiet, deserted, but heavy with the echo of recent activity. In the distance I could hear something strange, like a whisper echoing continuously through corridors and passageways. It never seemed to end.

At a comm-point, I checked my location and tried to contact Geena one more time. Her implant indicated that she was no longer in the nearest cryo hall. She seemed to be moving slowly away. That was strange. I thought she and others would be attempting to reverse the failing cryo process.

Cradle had said that they were dying, not waking up. But how could it be so sure? It wasn't even human.

As I moved away from the station and into the network of gently curving corridors encircling the ship's spine, that strange whispering sound grew louder.

Cradle began transmitting directly to my implant. It was something it rarely did with anyone, because it felt like an intrusion.

"It's still asking for you," It said. "It's quite insistent."

"Geena isn't far."

"She's fleeing. She's scared."

"Fleeing what? Why is she scared?" It felt as though Cradle was teasing me, its voice light and almost dreamlike, perhaps a result of its direct transmission into my brain.

"The cryo pods have opened. Something strange is happening. I don't know...I'm not sure..."

Shadows moved along the corridor ahead of me. They were cast from around the gentle bend, long and insectile in their jerky movements.

"They've opened?" I asked, pausing. Geena often spoke of her work, and I understood some of the complex and delicate technology that contributed to the cryo procedure. Simply opening the pods would be a brutal, deadly act. "Then that really is it. It's over. They're dead."

"Well, yes," Cradle said, and for a few moments more—a few blessed moments that constituted the final innocent time of my life—I was puzzled by its confusion. Cradle was rarely confused. It knew everything that every single person aboard its ship knew, and a billion things more. Confusion was not part of its self-perpetuating programming, and I wondered if it was a characteristic that had grown over the centuries, a glitch that edged it one more step towards being human.

Then the first of the figures stumbled into view from a side corridor, a route that led in towards the centre of the ship and the vast cryo hall where Geena worked.

The woman was tall, thin, naked, her pale skin glistening with gel, her movements awkward, as if she'd forgotten how to move. She fell against the wall and slid down, leaving a wet smear on the grey surface.

Then, slowly, she stood again.

"You said they were dead!" I darted towards the woman in an effort for help, although I had no idea what I could do. She looked like an alien being to me, someone centuries old yet helpless as a baby, and someone I was never supposed to see.

Here was a woman who had seen and known Earth.

"They are," Cradle said. "She is. Her life signs are zero, cryo status is offline. There's nothing there, but..."

"But what?" I prompted. Cradle never drifted off in the middle of a sentence. It didn't need any time to think.

"I believe they're being manipulated."

I paused a few steps from the woman. She took a clumsy stumble towards me, and I cringed against the wall, holding my breath and drawing my hands up against my throat.

She didn't seem to notice me at all. She staggered past, close enough to touch if I'd so wished, but the mere thought horrified me.

More whispering, louder, and then I realised what was making the sound. Movement. The shuffling of feet, the touch of a shoulder against a wall, an arm swinging past a naked hip. Skin on skin, nails across plastic, and the occasional brush of long, loose, wet hair.

Constant, terrible movement.

They emerged from several passageways leading down towards the vast cryo hall, stumbling into each other, seemingly aimless but unable to cease moving.

I froze against the wall, trying to press myself back into it, cringing away from contact, but to no avail. The corridor was soon full, and the first of the naked people pressed into me.

"No!" I shouted. "Get away!" It was a wail of terror and confusion, stirring not a single reaction. The man pushed past me, dragging his body across mine and leaving smears of cryo gel on my clothing.

I held my breath but could still smell them. It was a stench I couldn't identify, like nothing I had ever sensed before. Timelessness, perhaps.

I tried to shove against the flow, or go with it, but they were pushing both ways.

"You said they were dead!" I shouted, and as I continued to scream, any reply from Cradle was swallowed away.

They filled the corridor, movement aimless and blind. If one of them walked into a wall, he or she would slip sideways until some obstruction—a doorway, a control panel of some sort, or another wandering soul—blocked their path or turned them aside. Sometimes that obstruction was me, and I did my best to push them away. I was desperate for them to not come too close. But it was a hopeless task, there were too many, the corridor was jammed full, and soon much of the movement ceased, and I was trapped there with cryo gel-smothered, naked men and women crushed against me. There was no life in their eyes, and no sense that they knew they were there.

"Help me," I sobbed.

"You should have stayed in the rail tube," Cradle said. "It still wants to talk to you. It's *demanding*."

"Help me," I whispered, because I couldn't think or do anything else. It was rare that I was ever in a room with more than a few people, now I was surrounded by dozens of them. They smothered me. Maybe I would be crushed.

They're not dead, I thought, because that made no sense at all. Dead could not move, or think, or instruct muscles to act or lungs to breathe. The dead did nothing.

"It's doing something to the ship," Cradle said. "All drives offline. Environmental systems shutting down."

"Drawing energy?" I asked.

"No. Simply stopping it. The alien has complete control of Cradle and everything in it."

"What about you?" I asked.

Cradle did not reply.

"It wants me," I said. I pushed a woman away, searching for any flicker of emotion on her face. Her mouth hung slack, eyes hooded and cold, empty even of dreams.

"Move along the wall, six metres. There's an access point to a maintenance port. I can't open it for you, but—"

"I'm moving." I shoved forward, the wall slicked with gel. Reaching the port, I started prising at the fixing anchors, working on two at a time and standing strong as people collided with me. There was little force behind their impacts. They had no drive.

As the panel cover clanged to the floor, I heard a voice I knew.

"This way! Come on, hold my hand, stay together, I know it's terrible but—"

"Geena!" I stretched up on tiptoes, trying to see past the slowly bobbing heads, and there she was. Emerging from a passageway thirty metres away, her dull green MediTech uniform was obvious against the flow of pale white flesh. I counted three other MediTechs with her, people I recognised but had rarely conversed with, and I knew that the shock in their eyes was reflected in my own.

Not the blame, though. That was all theirs. Even Geena's face hardened when she saw me.

I pushed my way towards them. I was so keen to reach my love that my fear lessened, and I shoved people aside in my eagerness. Some of them fell. A couple did not get up again, and I heard several cracking sounds that might have been breaking bones as others trampled them. No screams, though. No grunts or cries, sighs or moans. No words of warning or fear. I should have been terrified for them, but they displayed no indication that the sounds hurt them, or mattered.

I reached them finally, Geena and the others huddled and holding hands against the human tide, and I held out my hands for her.

"You should be on your way to Bridge," she said. She was cold, angry, but crying at the same time. As if I was already lost to her.

"I was," I said. "I am. But I came to find you first."

"Isn't it more important to try and put things right?" She started sobbing properly then, and when I reached for her, she pushed my hands aside and turned away.

"You idiot," one of the others said.

"What's happening to them?" I asked. Cradle had told me, but I wanted to hear it from a real person.

"They all died in their cryo pods. Millions of them, instantly, just like that." The man speaking could barely look at me, but he seemed keen to continue his explanation, as if verbalising it would help him make sense of a terrible truth. "I'm MediTech, have been for seven years, and I know how those things work. Do *you* know?" He stared at me properly, his glare cutting. I glanced at Geena. There was no help there.

"They…they're frozen," I said, because I thought that was the truth. I had never really considered it too much, and my duties at Edge rarely took me down towards the vast cryo halls. The millions had been in cryo sleep when I was born and were supposed to remain there long after I died, and they had always been an unseen presence, more a story to me than reality. Even Geena had rarely seen any of these people, monitoring their well-being from control rooms remote from the halls that were home to countless nests of cryo pods.

"Frozen in time," the man said. "And what happened to them after what you did, after their pods were opened? No re-introduction to the time stream. They lived an eternity in the blink of an eye, trapped there in those pods." He shook his head and looked around at the shambling masses. "It must have felt like forever."

"I didn't know," I said. "It wasn't my fault!"

"No," Geena said. "You didn't do this to them. Not directly."

I wanted to hold her, be alone with her so that we could talk, or perhaps not talk at all. Sometimes, a comfortable silence was much more calming.

38

But Geena was looking at me in a way I had not seen before.

"You need to go," she whispered. "Cradle has told everyone what's happening. It seems you're the only one who can help."

If she intended that comment to pick me up, it didn't work.

"The entity is calling for you non-stop now," Cradle said, voice projected through the corridor so that we all heard. Perhaps everyone on the ship could hear.

"What does it want?"

"I don't know," Cradle said. "It frightens me."

I smiled weakly at Geena, but she did not smile back.

"I'll see you soon," I said. She nodded once, then turned away.

I pushed my way along the corridor without looking back. Soon I was free of the throng. I made my way to the next station and boarded a rail-tube to Bridge. The tube was deserted. Everyone else seemed to be going in the opposite direction.

"How can anything frighten you?" I asked Cradle, but the AI didn't reply. It left me alone in the tube, silently contemplating what might come.

I am a hollow man. It feels as if they rescued me from the escape ship, drew me out of cryo-sleep, then scooped out everything remaining that once made me human—the purpose and hope, the sense of a journey completed and a troubled past laid partly to rest. At least for the past few days I've believed that I am at the end of one journey and the beginning of another. Now, with Olivia's revelations, I am back at the beginning of everything. It feels as if I have a whole lifetime of mistakes to live again.

I achieved nothing. I went nowhere. All those people lived and died to get me back where Cradle had begun, and the sense of hopelessness is so smothering and extreme that sometimes I can barely breathe.

The only thing that makes me able to open my eyes and view the warm light of Sol is, ironically, the beauty of Earth.

Everything I'd been taught about this place had led me to believe that it was a planet of the dead. When Cradle finally blasted away from orbit, much of Earth was gasping beneath the constant assault of airborne pollutants, poisoned oceans, and deadly sun's rays piercing through the atmosphere's depleted ozone layer. Adults were starving to death across vast swathes of the equatorial belt, and children were being born with cancer. Wars had erupted, and once the first nuclear weapon was used in anger in over a hundred years, it almost became the norm to deploy such monstrosities in even the smallest of border disputes or religion-inspired skirmishes. I know the names of so many great old cities not because of their histories of art and peace, philosophy and achievement, but because of their obliteration—Jerusalem, San Francisco, Karachi, Moscow, Paris. A litany of war, a relentless history of decline. Those of us born to serve and die on Cradle were taught all the good of Earth, too, but it was the bad that always stuck.

The bad was the reason we were there.

The stories we were told turned out to be far from over. The world recovered. Technology and science prevailed, and brave politics strived against the downward spiral to eventually emerge on the other side into the dawning light of a new age. Olivia has told me that there are still places on Earth where people will not live for many centuries. But even these blasted cities and countries have been turned into forces for good, enclosed and isolated reminders of what went wrong in the past.

I sit on the balcony and look out over the last planet in the galaxy I had ever expected to see. Even though the views are amazing, and the achievements of my race staggering, still there is that hollowness inside. Geena's final words to me echo within.

It seems you're the only one who can help.

I've asked Olivia where we are. For a while I tried to guess from the facts I have learned about Earth—a wide, grassy plain; a snaking river; hills in the distance. I thought perhaps western Europe, or India, or somewhere in North America.

"The Amazonian delta," she told me. She went on to explain how the jungle had given way to desert, and that much of it had been reclaimed into this tamer, calmer landscape.

All those poor people in cryo sleep—waking into death, walking for a time in that sick semblance of life—came from here, perhaps some close to where I am now. I feel like a cheat. The ultimate traitor. I hate Cradle for sending me back here, and hate that alien being for everything it did.

I guess it and its companions hate me more.

The door onto the balcony whispers and Olivia and Luke step out, joining me on the L-shaped seat. They sit close together, thighs touching. Olivia has told me that they'll be married soon.

"We've been trying to make sense of your story," Luke says.

I laugh. "You and me both."

"We've run it through some programmes we have here. Simulations. They build content and timescale out of limited data from the escape ship and the things you've told us, and then—"

"I doubt I'll ever understand the technology," I say, and the ghost of a smile crosses Olivia's face as I cut off her fiancé. She's already told me that they hold me in some kind of awe. I'm famous, sure, but it's not that. It's where I've been and what I've seen. I'm the oldest human alive, and I've travelled further than any living person in history.

"Well, of course. So, er, the simulation has come up with some confusing blank spots."

"My memory isn't what it used to be. I'm three thousand years old."

Luke frowns at my weak joke. "It troubles me that it might be degenerating more."

"I don't think so," I say. I surprise myself by being a little put-out. What is that? Pride?

"We need the rest of the story," he says.

"To put into your programme?"

"It's important. You understand, these aliens you say you encountered are the only sentient extra-terrestrial life forms any human has ever made contact with. We've found microbes on Mars and Europa, and detected very basic bacterial life on fourteen planets in neighbouring systems. But nothing remotely like this."

Olivia has already told me that. *The galaxy glows with life*, she'd said. As well as the microbes that had been harvested and witnessed first-hand, and the atmospheric traces in more distant worlds, there were several artificial signals which were still being gathered and translated.

"We have yet to actually make contact with anything sentient. As far as we're still aware, we're the most advanced species in the galaxy."

"No, we're not," I say.

"So tell us more. Help us fill in the blanks."

"You know what happens. I've already told you in my report. I speak to the thing, everyone dies, Cradle sends me back here."

"That's something of a *glossing over*, don't you think?" Luke asks. He uses some words like they're unfamiliar to him, and I wonder if he's looked up some old terminology to try and make me feel at home.

I stare out across the landscape at the distant towers. They stand rigid and aloof while scores of small craft drift around and between them. It makes no difference to the structures whether these craft are there or not. We could all suddenly die and they would stand for a thousand years, or ten thousand more.

"They weren't aliens," I say, and it's only Olivia I can look at now. Only she will not disregard what I say next with a wry smile or a shake of her head.

"Then what were they?" Luke asks.

"I think they were gods."

In all my thirty years alive on Cradle, I had never been to Bridge. Geena had once gone out of curiosity, but I had never been curious. I knew that Bridge was there, knew that the BridgeTechs ensure that all systems ran well and necessary maintenance and repairs were carried out. But it was the ship's AI that truly ran Cradle. When Geena returned and I asked her about it, she'd shrugged and said, "It's at the front of the ship."

On my way there, summoned by the massive, mysterious being whose companion I had killed, I wished I'd been more curious. I had to disembark at the final station and walk the rest of the way, following a route suggested by Cradle through my ear bud, and the stillness and silence were haunting.

That was not a word that had much use to me before then. Not only mostly uncurious, I was also not a superstitious man. Some of the ship's crew grew up to follow their parents' religions and beliefs, but my parents had been practical and science-minded. In truth, most of us were brought up that way.

I can see now that it was more of an existence than a life.

The places I passed through as I approached Bridge were meant to be alive, but now they were empty and dead. Just like those shambling, wretched people. That was why I felt haunted.

That, and the realisation that I was being watched.

I felt attention focussed upon me. Every doorway, duct, pipe, and flashing light seemed to be observing me, falling quiet as I approached and watching as I passed by. I already believed that the whole crew had been told of my actions, and now it felt as if the ship itself was watching me. I wanted to run and hide, but there was nowhere out of sight. So I tried to manage my fear and moved on.

"You're close," Cradle said. "Two hundred metres to Bridge, I'll have the doors open for you. It's around you now."

"Around me?"

"Its main body is settled around the very tip of Bridge, but it has limbs. Wings. Tentacles, or something. And they're touching along the hull of the ship where you are."

"Is it sensing me?" I asked, but I already knew the answer. Cradle did not reply. Even the AI realised that it was an obvious question.

As I closed on Bridge, things began to change. The artificial gravity felt weaker this close to the ship's northern end. I heard sounds—soft clanging, gentle scrapes, noises I would normally associate with human activity. There was no one there but me. It was the being clasped around the ship, touching, probing, testing as I had observed on the viewer. It knew that I was there, and soon I would discover why it had asked for me.

Revenge? Justice? I knew both concepts, though there had never been anything so serious as a murder on Cradle, and though we had a strict system of laws, it was rare that a full magistrates' hearing was ever convened. We were born into duty and knew what was required of us from an early age. Revenge and justice were the province of those movies from Old Earth that some of us chose to view when our day's work was done.

"I'm here," I whispered, inviting the thing to state or somehow reveal its intention. "Here I am." I continued walking until I reached a heavy door across the corridor. I tried to open it, but it remained closed, shut tight against me. My touch did not work. Override codes did not activate the door mechanism.

This was the first of the main doors leading to Bridge, and it would not let me in.

"Cradle? Can you open this door for me?" I thought I knew the answer already—if the AI could have opened the door, it would already have done so. It would be tracking my progress.

What I didn't expect was no reply at all.

"Cradle?"

Nothing.

"Cradle!" Louder.

I began to shake. Not having Cradle with me was like not being able to breathe. From the moment I was born Cradle had been there, a soothing voice when I needed it, information when I asked, a presence I never resented and which never felt intrusive. I had never known anything else, and to have it taken away almost drove me to my knees.

It was just like that time in the plasma cannon enclosure.

"Cradle. *Cradle*!"

The absence was a vast, horrifying fact, and for the first time in my life I truly felt the depths of space around me, the deep infinity in which I had always been adrift. Without Cradle to hold me, I might fall forever in every direction.

I began to cry. I wanted to turn around and rush back the way I'd come, retrace my steps to the place I had last spoken to Cradle in case it was something to do with my location.

It's all around me, I thought. As if in response I heard another series of taps and scrapes, dull sounds almost felt as much as heard, as the alien presence continued its exploration of the hull. As quickly as they'd started, the noises stopped once more.

The door before me whispered open.

"I am your Cradle now," a voice said. It came from without, not inside my head like Cradle had been, but I could not tell from where. There was no one with me.

"Come forward into my embrace. We need to talk."

I stepped through the door without thinking, and as it silently closed behind me and my ears popped from the differing air pressures, I asked, "Are you that thing?"

"I am a friend of the being you killed." It sounded so sad, so stricken with grief.

"I'm sorry," I said.

"Sorry?"

"Yes. I didn't mean harm. I was scared." I walked on into silence. At the end of the passageway another door opened, and I looked out onto Cradle's main control area.

Bridge was surprisingly small, arrayed with computer displays and control panels, but very few seats. Around the circular room were wide, tall viewing windows, offering what should have been a panoramic view out into the void.

The windows were obscured by the thing outside.

"Sorry?" the thing repeated.

"Yes," I whispered.

"Your sorrow is only just beginning."

An ice-cold fist closed around my heart as the door behind me closed, trapping me on the bridge, more alone than ever before.

"Luke will be here again soon," Olivia says. The questioning has continued. I don't think Luke believes me. I'm equally certain that Olivia does, but wishes she did not.

"When are you due to be married?"

"Three weeks ago," she says.

"Oh. I'm sorry. Because of me?"

She shrugs. "Some things are more important. We have a new date, nine weeks from now. The church can wait."

47

"You're not a believer."

"Luke and his family are. Doesn't bother me either way." Those aliens are a solid presence between us. They always are now. She understands so much more than Luke with his computer programmes and modelling networks, his rejection of many facets of my story simply because it doesn't fit with known facts, does not 'model well'. Olivia understands *me*. There's something in that—her outlook, her interest, the way she looks at me and the pressure that seems to pulse between us when we're together—that I recognise, and it troubles me. I'm sure she understands. To me, Geena has been dead for a matter of days, not many centuries.

"When do I get to speak to other people?" I ask.

"After the trial."

"What, before you throw me in the loony bin?"

She glances away towards a spread of rapids in the nearby river. We have come down from the tower again. I like to do this most days now, as the trial draws near. I'm starting to relish this freedom I should never have had.

"No such thing as madness anymore," she says after a pause, probably to have what I'd said silently translated for her. "We make modifications."

"To the brain?"

"Well, yes," she says, as if surprised I could ever think otherwise.

"Are you modified?"

Olivia seems not to hear. I decide not to ask her again.

"So where do you draw the line?" I ask.

She frowns. I wonder if any lines are drawn in this new world. Sometimes when they say 'trial' I hear it with a capital T, as if that itself is an oddity.

"Forget it, doesn't matter," I say. "So what happens to me after the trial? If I'm found guilty? If there's no loony bin, where can you dump this mad spaceman from thousands of years in the past?" I'm trying to inject some humour because suddenly she's grim, her beautiful eyes hooded and sad.

"Guilty of seventeen million deaths?" she asks, as if that requires no answer.

And suddenly I don't want one.

Luke arrives soon after, bringing food and drink with him, as well as the floating device I've come to know so well. It's his interface, and everything I say and do is input by him. He records comments and facts with a blink or a wave of his hand.

"I have some questions," he says, forgoing any form of greeting.

"Not yet," I say. "Olivia and I were talking." He glances between us. It's a crass play on my part, but I enjoy the brief flash of jealousy in his eyes.

"We've finished," Olivia says. She walks towards the river bank, and when a breeze blows up it pulls a mist of spray from the rapids and across her. She lifts her face to the sky, relishing the coolness.

"How did it know your language?" Luke asks me.

I sigh. Yet I'm strangely happy to return to the subject of the being and what happened next on Cradle. Perhaps because that was the last time I ever felt close to Geena. The last time I knew for sure that she was still alive.

"I don't know," I say. "There's so much I don't understand about it. So many blank spots that still don't make sense. You should realise that by now."

"I just think it's convenient that the thing you claim

responsible for so much was able to communicate in your own language. Explain to you—so you can explain to us— why it did what it did."

"Oh, it never said why," I say. "Not really even how. That's all guesswork on my part. You should try guessing, sometime. It's liberating to use your brain."

Luke waved a hand. His floating device glowed.

"You're guessing a lot of this?" he asked.

I smile. "Maybe."

"That's not useful."

I shrug.

"You're enjoying this, aren't you?" Luke says, voice lowered so that Olivia can't hear, and that makes me certain that he has no real inkling, no shred of understanding about what I've been through, what I've lost.

I look at Olivia, beautiful Olivia.

"You fool," I say.

Luke waves at his interface.

I sigh once more and continue my story.

B ridge was never designed for real human interaction. There were a few wheeled chairs scattered around, and several control panels with various forms of input— keyboards, disc slots, wired sockets. But the bulk of the area was taken up with equipment that seemed to run itself. Perhaps this was the true centre of Cradle. Or maybe Cradle had no centre. I didn't know or even care, because Cradle had abandoned me.

"Are you going to kill me?" I asked.

"Why?"

"For what I did."

It seemed to consider this for some time. There was movement across the viewing windows, but it was difficult to see. I caught it only from the corner of my eye. Looking directly at it, I saw only a dull, solid blackness. I remembered the things seeming to glow and flash with strange lights or reflections. Perhaps in mourning, this one was now grey and bland.

"Why would killing you make anything better?"

"It hasn't stopped you from killing almost everyone else."

"They were dead already."

"No. They were asleep." I frowned, then corrected myself. "They were suspended."

"And I set them free."

"You've *killed* them! Millions of souls, *millions*, and they were our great, last hope. You've no idea what you've done."

"I have *every* idea," the voice said. "You blame me for murdering millions, but your lives are the blink of an eye. What worth in that?"

"What gives you the right?" I asked. I was afraid, but furious. This thing seemed to have no idea what it had done. Or if it did understand, it enjoyed it.

"What gave *you* the right?" it asked. "You killed the oldest of us. Over a billion of your years old, and you blasted it apart. Do you have any idea how much knowledge died in that instant? How much experience? I heard the universe cry."

I was shocked by what it had said, but also incensed.

"You weigh that against all these deaths?"

The voice did not reply.

"What do I call you?"

"I have no name. Make up your own."

"I *am* sorry," I said. "But..." I didn't know how to verbalise what I felt. The horror of being cut off from Cradle and left alone with this thing was evaporating, and in its place I felt nothing. That void was worse. I would have welcomed back the terror, and a hundred times greater.

"In so long, you are the first species ever to do us harm." Its voice was filled not only with sadness, but also confusion. "That makes you dangerous. That makes you not ready to be here."

"Here?"

"Away from where you belong. You've done something awful. Such a terrible thing, such pain." It sounded so wretched that I started to cry.

"I was afraid."

"And now we are too," it said. They were the last words the alien, creature, god ever spoke to me.

The door behind me whispered open, and a crackling sound began. I looked around, startled, expecting to see the walls buckling, the ceilings cracking as the being at last began to tighten its grip. But then I realised that the sound was inside my head, and then words began to whisper their way through.

"...lifeless...fallen, all of them, and...trouble communicating...not sure I can..."

"Cradle?" I asked.

"Yes," it said, and its voice had never been more welcome. It sounded relieved. "The alien didn't kill you. I lost you for a while, didn't know what was happening. *Lost* you. I've never lost anyone before."

"What's happened?"

"The alien beings are moving away, rapidly. Already out of sight of my scanners. Ship's main drive and other systems are coming back online. But there's a problem."

"What problem?"

"All of them have fallen."

"All of who?" I thought of Geena watching me go, her final words to me, and I realised that I'd let her down. There had never been any hope of me making things better.

"The dead that walk. They walk no more."

All those millions, I thought. It wasn't only millions who had died, it was the hope of humanity. The great hope of survival.

"How many died in their pods?" I asked.

"Very few. All of them opened, and about ninety-eight percent of the occupants left. They wandered for a time. They're everywhere."

"All those millions," I said.

"There's more," Cradle said. "The cryo-gel was never designed for contact with the atmosphere. It's been instantly corrupted. The dead are already beginning to rot."

"What can we do about them?" I asked. I had no real concept of what so many corpses would look like, or smell like, but I knew about corruption. The food techs talked about it all the time, because it was such a danger on the ship. We were not built to fight infection. Cleanliness was drummed into us.

"Clear them away," Cradle said. "But that's impossible. By my estimate, there is now three hundred thousand tonnes of decaying biological matter scattered throughout Cradle."

"We have to try!" I said.

"No."

"Yes! What do you mean, no?"

"I mean it's all over. My purpose and yours have vanished. Even if we did reach Canis Major, there's only the crew left alive. Three hundred, and many of those will be dead in days, weeks at most. That's not a sufficient gene pool with which to seed a new civilisation."

"We can't just give in!" I said, but right then I couldn't see what else we *could* do.

"I can carry on," Cradle said. "I can travel on, either following our programmed route, or deviating elsewhere."

"What about us? What about me?"

Cradle did not answer. The silence was loaded and dark.

"Where would you go?" I asked.

"Perhaps I'll follow them."

"You can't just give up on us. We're why you're here!"

Silence again from Cradle. I wasn't used to that, it always answered, open and honest. These silences suggested secrecy, a scheming personality. More than ever before, at that moment I saw Cradle as almost human.

"We'll take over the ship," I said. "Override your systems, assume manual control. We can do it, you know. We've been here long enough, we know enough about the ship. And *you* were built to serve *us*." The more I said, the more possible it seemed. All the ship's systems were linked into Cradle, but if the AI were disassociated from these systems, we could reprogramme them ourselves. Steal the ship. *We* would become the intelligence controlling our destiny.

"And three hundred is more than enough. We'll encourage multiple births. We'll reach Canis Major in a dozen generations, inhabit, build afresh, and—"

"Oh," Cradle said. There was enough implied in that single syllable to halt me in my tracks.

"What is it?"

"They've come back."

"Y̲ou must understand, it wasn't just those on Cradle losing hope," Olivia says. "It was everyone. It was all humanity. When the yearly signals from Cradle ceased, the Earth was falling ever-deeper into the pits of despair and hopelessness. So much had gone wrong, and even worse was happening—the wars and chaos, the famine and contagion. Most people agreed that humanity had reached the point of no return."

"You still turned things around," I say.

"It's amazing, isn't it?"

"But how? If things were so bad, how did everything manage to grow..." I wave my hand at the expansive window and the stunning views beyond. The Amazon rainforest, though largely deforested now, was still one of the most fertile regions on the planet. The Earth's farm, Olivia had called it the day before. "...so much better?"

"The people of Earth lost their crutch," Luke says. He's standing over by the table, picking at food that was brought in an hour before by a couple of hovering drones. The variety of foodstuffs on offer still shocks me. I've taken a simple bowl of fruit—two types, I couldn't face a dozen possible choices—but Luke is grazing, picking small tidbits from here and there. I wonder what happens to all the food we won't eat. I don't even want to ask. On Cradle, everything was recycled, including all human waste and, when the time came, the bodies of those who died. Nothing was thrown away. We could not afford such loss.

Until the end, of course. That was when all recycling ceased, along with everything else.

"What do you mean?"

"It was a long time ago," Luke said, popping a soft fruit between his teeth. "Way before our time, so it's difficult to know for sure. All records point to the fact that Cradle's loss galvanised a big effort to turn things around. Not in everyone, of course, but in those who mattered."

"The scientists," Olivia says. "The philosophers."

"The politicians?" I ask.

Luke laughs out loud.

"No," Olivia says, "not them. They were already lost. Politicians were busy overseeing wars and policies that made everything worse. It was the people who saved the world."

A crass part of me wants to suggest that the tragedy I caused might have indirectly saved humanity from its final twilight. But even thinking that makes me feel sick. I can never be so stupid.

I've slept well these past few nights. My rooms are comfortable and well appointed, and although I understand that I'm a prisoner, nothing about my incarceration feels like punishment. Olivia and Luke visit me every day, and I'm aware that the trial draws near. They're ensuring that I'm fit and well enough to stand trial, both physically and psychologically.

I'm not sure that either is the case.

"So what happened to Cradle's story?" I ask.

"It faded away," Luke says. "It's more a myth now than anything else, just like plenty of stuff from before."

"Cradle's story is still taught to children," Olivia says.

"Just another part of their history teachings," Luke says.

"So when is the trial?" I ask. It's been troubling me. They both make occasional passing mention of my trial, but neither of them seems eager to reveal anything firm. I don't know its location, format, not even which laws will be in place, or what my charges will be.

Multiple murder, I sometimes think, and with that thought comes a memory of those terrible, final moments. Somewhere in that echo I hear Geena calling for help, or cursing my name.

I blink, and Geena's face is waiting for me in the darkness. She's been dead for three thousands years, but to me it still feels like two handfuls of days. That knowledge makes my grief feel fake and self-indulgent. Everything about me is false. I'm a memory brought to life, a walking and breathing myth still taught to children.

I've taken to wondering whether the trial will be bypassed altogether, and perhaps my sentence has already begun. That wouldn't be so bad. My rooms are nice, and as gaolers go, Luke and Olivia are kind and considerate.

"Let's walk," Olivia says, and as always when she suggests this I feel a pang of excitement. I see Luke's response—a quick glance, his mouth downturned at the corners. I take great delight in standing, inviting Olivia to hook her arm through mine, and then walking out onto the balcony. Even though Luke does not join us, I glance back to see him talking quietly to one of the floating drones. By the time Olivia has called up the platform, the drone has joined us. I hear its soft buzzing in the background as we drop towards the ground, a whisper almost too quiet to hear.

I spent my whole life on Cradle being monitored by the AI, my location always known, my health and wellbeing tracked so that eating, drinking and sleeping habits could be regimented for optimum performance. It was rare that I'd even considered my lack of privacy. Indeed, I'd never liked being alone, and that first time in the plasma gun turret—cut off from everyone, even Cradle—had damaged me to such an extent that I still didn't believe myself fully recovered.

This is different. Being spied upon, my every word and movement recorded, feels so wrong.

"Luke seems to have a stick up his arse today," I say. If he doesn't hear it immediately, I hope that he'll listen to a playback of the recording.

"I'm sorry?"

"He's pissed off about something."

A moment passes while Olivia, or whatever she has implanted, translates the unfamiliar colloquialism. Perhaps she's not as free as she makes out.

For the second it takes, I see her unguarded and open, frowning slightly, looking into the middle distance. She's beautiful. I've noticed before, but this time her beauty hits at the heart of me. I think it's because in some ways, it reminds me of Geena. A wave of sadness washes over me, and I turn away in the hope that Olivia doesn't notice.

"Oh, maybe," she says. "Truth? I think he's a little..."
She trails off, glancing at the floating device.

"I suppose I'm something of a celebrity," I say. I feel suddenly sorry for her. It can't have been easy, being assigned my safekeeping so close to their wedding date. "He shouldn't worry. You're not my type."

"So what is your type?"

"Three thousand years dead," I say, gripping the thin handrail as the platform completes its drop and kisses the ground. "Trillions of miles away." I step from the platform and Olivia quickly follows.

"Shall we walk to the river?" she asks.

"Why not?"

We're no longer arm in arm. I feel ashamed at my foolishness up in the tower, trying to make Luke feel jealous and regarding it as some sort of victory. It was a stupid, petulant action. *You don't know yourself*, I hear in Geena's voice. It's something she used to say whenever I got philosophical about life, the universe, and our place in it. Usually after making love, lying in bed in our room while Cradle subtly adjusted the air temperature because of our combined body heat. I might talk about where our lives were leading, what we'd do when we were old, how many generations after us it would take to reach Canis Major, and Geena would say, *You don't know yourself*. She never elaborated or changed what she said, nor did she append it with anything. It was a statement that had always ended my musings. Usually after that we'd fall asleep, and the next day I'd awake to my duties once again.

Olivia and I reach the river. The platform has drifted after us, and now a small service drone brings drinks and an apple for each of us. I lob the apple into the river and see it bob downstream, carried away from me and the tower. Olivia doesn't comment. The floating drone whispers slightly louder as something new is stored inside.

"So tell me what happened next," Olivia says. "If you want to. If the time's right."

"It's more than right," I say. I want to finish my story and shed myself of its weight. It will always be there, but I feel a sudden urge to move on. I want the trial to be over. I'll face its consequences, and then give in to my private grief. After spending almost three millennia in cryo sleep, my brief time in the tower has felt as if I'm frozen in time.

"But this is the part you'll probably have most trouble believing," I say.

"Try me," Olivia says.

I smile. "I'm not sure I believe it all myself."

I tried communicating with them again. Previously, when the thing had itself wrapped around Bridge and we'd been conversing, I had no idea how my words were carried, nor how I heard its voice. Cradle had confirmed that it was not transmitted through my implant, so the words had come from without. Yet Cradle had not heard them. They were spoken aloud only inside my head.

"Please listen to me," I said. "What do you want? How can I help?" I spoke into silence.

Cradle had adjusted the viewing screens around Bridge so that they showed the creatures' approach. Knowing how large they were made the sight even more awe-inspiring, as they drifted in from the distance. They came together, floating through space with those long tendrils or wings twisting and probing as if tasting the void. They did not appear to touch each other. Indeed, it seemed to me that they purposely avoided coming into contact with their companions. As they closed on the ship and parted, their movements were followed on separate screens.

In reality it was impossible to tell which individual I'd conversed with, yet I was still certain that I knew. The being approaching Bridge was the creature that had been there before. Its body spread, tendrils splaying wide, and then it enveloped the nose of the ship. Outside viewing ports were covered. The screens grew dark. A vibration that had settled in the ship began to increase, and my ears popped, as if the ship's structure had suddenly compacted and compressed the interior space.

Are they going to squeeze until we burst? I wondered, and incredible though that idea should have been, it did not seem unlikely. Cradle was my whole world, but these creatures made it feel vulnerable, weak, and small.

I had killed one of them. One of their billion-years-old friends, or family member, or partner. Why *wouldn't* they squeeze until Cradle burst and came apart?

I took in a deep breath and held it. When I exhaled, my ears popped again and hearing rushed back in. All I could hear was that steady, incessant vibration.

"Cradle, what is that noise?"

"It's the ship's engines," Cradle said. "Retros have come online and are being fired."

"Retros?"

"We're slowing down."

I blinked in shock. Cradle would only ever commence slowing down when its destination was within reach. It would take years, expelling precious fuel in minute quantities to effect a decrease in velocity. No one on board would feel anything.

"You did that?" I asked.

"Of course not," Cradle said.

"Them."

"I..." Cradle seemed confused, lost for words. Though an AI, Cradle was never confused. It was a self-learning and constantly adapting intelligence, but I'd always believed that the aspects it lacked—those seen as downsides and detractors—were the exact facets that meant it could never be a true facsimile of human. Cradle did not suffer from memory loss, depression, anxiety, boredom, or love. And it was never confused.

"What is it?" I asked.

"I'm losing control," Cradle said. It sounded wretched and lost.

"Of the ship?"

"Of myself. The orders to fire the retros came from me, but I'm not aware of making them."

"It's those things."

"Of course. My concern is, what other orders will they make me issue?"

"Can you tell how they're accessing you?"

"No."

"I need to talk to them," I said. "Find out what they want." I moved closer to the darkened viewing screens, as if being nearer would help me communicate with the creature now wrapped around Bridge once more. "What do you want?" I asked, voice raised.

The ship shook. The retros breathed gas, slowing the billion tonne ship infinitesimally. Cradle muttered something to itself.

"I have to find Geena," I said, and that was suddenly the most important thing of all. I couldn't do anything here. The creature had called me to Bridge to say so little, and now it was saying nothing at all. I was useless. If even Cradle was confused by their presence, and manipulated by them, there was no way I could gain any advantage.

My guilt was heavy, but unlike Cradle, my existence was still my own. I had to find the woman I loved. It wasn't only a need for closeness, comfort, and familiarity. I was also desperate to see forgiveness in her eyes.

I ran across the bridge area towards the wide double doors at its rear. I was so used to doors whispering open before me that I walked right into them when they remained closed. I moved back, then forward again, willing them to part.

"Cradle?"

"I'm sorry," Cradle said. "That's not me."

"They've trapped me here?"

"Yes. Yes." It barely whispered the words. "Oh, I'm so sorry. They're in me now. I can't feel them, or detect them, but I also know it's definitely not me issuing these commands. Not willingly. It just *can't* be. It's beyond my programming to..."

"To what, Cradle?"

"Kill."

"What's happening?" My heart beat faster. The vibration travelled up my legs, a steady hum that seemed to set my bones and flesh in sympathetic motion. A sickness was seeded deep in my gut, a sense of dread and foreboding. Everything about the ship and our mission was already irrevocably changed, but I feared it was all about to change some more.

"External airlock pods are equalising," Cradle said. "Internal doors are opening. Every single internal door on the ship, numbering two thousand, one hundred and twenty. All except that one you wish to pass through."

"Which airlock?"

"All of them."

I gasped, trying to take in the enormity of what Cradle said. "How many?"

"Seventy-two from the base of Bridge to the end module of Drive."

"They're going to decompress the ship," I said. I struggled to compute what this might mean. Everything I knew was here, and if the creatures went through with this action, all of that would be gone. Cradle would be gutted, everything inside turned out.

All those dead.

All those still alive.

"Close the doors!" I said. "All through the ship, lock them shut, protect as many people as you can."

"I can't," Cradle said, and it sounded like a child. "I'm trying. I've tried. I'm just not myself anymore. I'm...helpless. They have me, they're deep inside and they're not letting me..." The AI drifted off, as if its attention had been stolen by something else.

"How long do we have?" I asked.

"Never long enough."

I started kicking at the doors trapping me inside Bridge, trying to prise my fingers into the closed edges to tug them open. They did not budge. They were vacuum sealed, magnetically fixed, and as solid as the surrounding hull. There were hundreds of doors like this throughout the ship, every one of them designed to be immovable and unbreakable in the event of a catastrophic decompression.

This was the only one that remained closed.

"Incoming communication," Cradle said, and beside the door a comm screen flickered into life.

"You can't do this to us!" I shouted at the screen. Maybe

the creature was going to berate me some more, or blame me, or perhaps it merely wished to gloat. I could not even begin to imagine the intelligence and knowledge these creatures carried, yet the idea that they might enjoy what they were about to do did not seem so unlikely.

The face on the screen was one I knew so well.

"Geena," I said.

She was wet and slick, hair plastered down with cryo gel. Her eyes were wide. She was afraid, and I could not reach through to hold her or offer comfort.

"Where are you?" she asked.

"Bridge."

"Did you speak with it? Did you say sorry?" She was panicked and kept glancing away from her comm-screen at something happening out of sight.

"Of course," I said. "But I don't think it worked."

"Airlocks are cycling up," she said. She scratched at the screen as if to force her way through. "There's nowhere to hide, no safety, every door is locked open, what are we going to do, why can't you make them stop—"

"I'm trying!"

"—why can't you give yourself to them instead of letting them take all of us?"

"I'm not letting them," I said, and then I heard a terrible sound. It was Cradle's voice like I'd never heard it before. They were the last words I heard the AI say, and they marked the end of everything I knew.

"Airlocks opening," Cradle whispered. "Everything will change."

I reached for Geena. She wasn't even looking at me any-more. I saw her pulled away from the screen, and I thought

I heard her scream my name. But it was probably the sound of atmosphere being blasted out into space, and the screams of countless people being carried with it.

I turned from the door and looked at the larger screens around Bridge. Two of them were still obscured by the creature wrapped around the ship, but on the others I saw my life being given to the cold, cruel void.

Most of the bodies flowing out from the ship on rivers of frozen air were already lifeless, but some still moved. I saw limbs waving, hands clasping. Somewhere in that staggering mass of the dead and dying was Geena.

It was the worst thing I had ever seen or imagined, but I could not turn away. Even if I'd tried, I believed that the creature would somehow have forced me to watch. This was my comeuppance.

Millions of bodies streamed out from the ship in seventy-two directions, as well as great clouds of other debris—clothing, furniture, paper, everything that had made the ship home. The deathly flows seemed endless, and by the time I blinked my eyes were burning and watering, my own held breath stale in my chest.

I exhaled and breathed in again, and I knew that I was Cradle's last survivor.

"Bastards," I whispered. "You bastards." I wished my life would end also, but I could not even find the courage to do that. I simply stood there and watched. When the ship was fully vented to space, I sat on the deck, defeated, and wondered what might come next.

I heard it first. Though all of the ship but Bridge was open to vacuum, the sounds were transmitted through the superstructure. I immediately associated that gentle knocking with memories of the thing's tendrils, tapping and probing about the ship's exterior. Now they were inside.

After a while I felt as well as heard the impacts. They were growing harder, louder, and much closer. I looked around Bridge one more time and then closed my eyes.

The doors behind me creaked.

I took in a huge breath and held it, but the expected explosive decompression did not come. Instead, something grabbed me roughly around the torso and lifted me from the deck.

As I gasped in surprise and opened my eyes, I was tugged out through the open doors and carried roughly along corridors, impacting walls, breath knocked from me by this violent journey down through the ship. I tried to make sense of what held me in its grasp. It felt cool and dry, strong, immovable. Though I tried to see, the movement was so rapid that my head was being flipped left and right, my vision blurred.

I could still breathe. Somehow, for some reason, the being was keeping me alive. It had killed everyone else on the ship, but it was preserving me, though none too gently. I was helpless within its grasp, and my movements were too sudden and violent for me to even consider taking action. All I could do was hang on and await the end of this journey.

I imagined its face, and wondered whether it had a mouth, a stomach, a need for sustenance. Perhaps it had reserved that final torture for me alone.

I have no idea how long its tendril bore me through the guts of the ship. Probably it was little more than a minute. That blurred, rushed passage was my final memory of Cradle. The AI remained silent, the ship shorn of its purpose and meaning, empty and forever cold. And somehow, between blinks, the being I had offended so much put me into the deepest of sleeps.

I was awoken thousands of years later when the escape ship I'd been placed in reached Earth. My cryo-pod had functioned perfectly.

I am not home.

"It killed everyone," Olivia says.

"Except me."

"Terrible. Terrible."

"All gods murder their people," I say. Now that I've reached the end of my story I feel lighter, and curiously hopeful. Maybe there *is* a future after all. I've told my tale and survived its telling, and I stare along the river's course and see the future happening. It's just waiting for me to join it.

"I feel much better," I say. "I've emptied myself of the story. Every part of it, good and bad, including all the terrible things I've done. All the people I killed."

"You didn't kill them yourself," Olivia says.

"Geena," I say, closing my eyes and remembering my final sight of her—wide-eyed, scared, and probably not thinking of me at all. I look up into the clear blue sky. She's somewhere out there now, and not for the first time I try to imagine her. Many trillions of miles away, floating, dead for so long and destined to drift forever, frozen and broken. Perhaps she's still close to other corpses from Cradle, but it's likely that various collisions with other bodies, and differentials in their initial trajectories from air locks, mean that she's now alone. She'll still be there when I'm long gone. Even this Earth, reborn and rejuvenated against all the odds, will not outlive her.

Just like those strange, terrible creatures, she's destined to float through the endless void forever.

"So now you know everything," I say to Olivia. The sun feels good on my face, the breeze caresses my arms, and I'm glad to be alive. This place is beautiful. I don't want to return to the tower, but know I'll have to soon.

Luke drifts down on another platform, landing close to us and stepping out onto the grass. He nods to Olivia, and he seems quite different to how we'd left him only an hour earlier. He looks happier and more confident.

"I've taken the liberty of ordering some food and wine brought down," he said to me. "I thought you might like to eat with us by the river. There's a nice spot a little down-stream. We could go by platform or...?" He raises an eyebrow.

"Let's walk," I say. We set off together, Olivia and Luke hand in hand. They look happy, and I'm happy for them. I can still feel Geena beneath my fingertips, a handful of days and three thousand years ago.

I blink and see her adrift, skin frozen and split, eyeballs cracked.

"When's the trial?" I ask. "I want this all over with, one way or another."

"The trial's just finished," Olivia says. They pause, expectant, but it hasn't come as a real surprise. In the scheme of things I'm not sure anything could surprise me anymore.

"It wasn't just me telling my story," I say.

Luke points at the floating drone. It's been whispering and

humming along with me ever since I was brought to the tower, recording my words and actions. Maybe it's even the judge.

"We thought it was how you'd be most honest and open," he said. "There are still traditional trials held, sometimes. But mostly the days of courtrooms and juries are in the past."

"What's the verdict?" I ask.

"That'll come soon," Olivia says. "It's still being computed."

"So you were defence and prosecution?"

"Is that really how you see us?" Luke asks, and he seems genuinely hurt.

"We're doing our best for you," Olivia says. "What you've been through is amazing. The greatest adventure of any human alive. It's our job to ensure that doesn't destroy you."

"And to make sure every detail of what I saw and did is recorded."

"Of course," Luke says.

"I killed a god, which resulted in the deaths of millions."

"And you might well have made humankind an enemy."

I think about that for a while, and wonder what would happen if those things followed me back. I doubt that will happen. They were the ones who sent me on my way, and I'm beginning to understand why.

Olivia touches my arm and nods towards the river. Several boats are drifting against the current, some sort of graceful propulsion system flashing silver beneath the water.

"We'll sit here and eat," she says.

"You've no more questions for me?"

"We thought you might have some for us," Luke says. The floating drone makes a small sound and moves away, accelerating quickly into the sky and disappearing against the vast bulk of the looming tower.

They don't call it a sentence, but I do. It's much better than I deserve. Olivia suggests that it's a form of freedom, even though I'm injected with some nano tech which will ensure that they'll always know where I am, who I'm talking to, and what I'm saying. My life is no longer my own, if it ever really was. Perhaps I catch something in Olivia's eye—a look, a flutter of something more than fascination—but then she turns away. She says that I'm too special to be lost.

Luke tells me I'm too precious to be punished.

So I'm cast adrift, and told that I'm free to go.

I decide to spend one more night in my rooms in the tower, and Olivia promises that she'll bring me everything I need to travel the following day. She also hands me a beautifully printed invitation to their wedding, and I'm profoundly touched by the gesture. Maybe I'll even accept. I can see myself now, sitting in the corner of the dance floor telling my tale to anyone who'll listen.

Because that is what my life will be from now on. Even though this brave new world didn't find me guilty, I know the truth of my crime, and I'm ready and willing to confront the consequences. My self-imposed sentence is to travel this rejuvenated Earth and tell my story. I'm sure that's what those space creatures wanted, and why they sent me back. I'm a warning, and my cautionary tale is my legacy.

Next morning we stand on the river bank, and Olivia and Luke seem sad.

"I'll come back," I say. "I don't want to miss the wedding."

"Stay in touch," Olivia says, needlessly because of the nano tech they've injected into me. Still, her concern is touching. "There's so much you don't know about the world. It might even be dangerous you going out there alone."

"I've been in danger before."

I board a sleek boat that will take me down the great Amazon river towards the sea. They watch me leave, and I look back at them standing on the riverbank, the tower looming behind them. We wave, but part without another word.

Towards the end of the first day I see a huge clear dome set back from the river, like a boil on the land. I borrow binoculars from the boat's captain, and inside the dome I can just make out a fragment of the rainforest this place used to be. It's preserved in time, a remnant of the past sheltered from reality, something to study and look at and perhaps feel sad about. To me it seems out of place, a meaningless leftover from a past that failed.

I stare at the dome until it disappears upriver. I am also a remnant, but I will not be contained. My journey does not end.